coping with
Loss and Grief

An imprint of Om Books International

'Stop licking my nose, Scamper!' Yelled little Oliver. 'And please get off, I can't get out of bed with you on top of me,' he laughed.

Oliver wondered why neither Daddy nor Grandma had come to wake him up today. Oliver's grandmother was his best friend and he felt his happiest best when he started his day with her loving cuddle!

She had been ill lately and Daddy had been waking him up each morning, but this morning seemed different.

'Come on, Scamper! Let's see what's going on.'

Oliver came down for breakfast, with Scamper at his heels. He was surprised to see his Aunt Sophie there.

'Good morning, Aunt Sophie! Are Jack and Nora here, too?' Oliver asked excitedly. Nora and Jack were his cousins.

'Good morning, Oliver,' said Aunt Sophie hugging him warmly. 'No, the children are not here with me.' Oliver could sense sadness in her tone.

`Finish your breakfast, darling,´ she added softly.
`I´ll drop you to the school bus today.´

Oliver was very puzzled.

`Where are Mommy and Daddy?' He asked, as he ate his breakfast.

`They've taken Grandma to see the doctor, darling. They'll all be back soon.'

'Is Grandma alright?' Oliver was suddenly very worried about his grandmother.

'Don't you worry, Oliver,' said Aunt Sophie, as she walked him to the waiting school bus. 'The doctor just wants to make Grandma feel better. I'll see you after school, all right?'

Oliver left for school. But he worried about Grandma.

He missed her company.

She and Oliver walked Scamper together every day.
They baked blueberry muffins together.
She told him bedtime stories.

`I hope Grandma gets better soon,´ he
thought to himself in class.

He longed to tell her stories about his friends and his school. Nothing seemed fun without her!

When Oliver returned from school, the house was filled with people. All his uncles, aunts and neighbours had come over to visit. The house was full of flowers, too. People walked in endlessly to meet his parents, and they brought more flowers. It seemed like some celebration, yet no one was happy.

Oliver was very happy to see everyone, but there were no children around. He could not see Grandma either. And although everyone hugged Oliver, and Mommy and Daddy never left sight of him, he couldn't see Grandma.

Oliver was very puzzled.

That night after everyone had left, Daddy and Mommy sat down to talk to Oliver.

`I haven't seen Grandma all day,' Oliver said. `Is she still with the doctor? Why were there so many people visiting us today?'

He had so many questions to ask!

'Oliver, Grandma's gone on a grand new adventure,' said Mommy with tears in her eyes.

'Can I go with her?' he whispered softly.

'No, Oliver. Grandma has to go alone. She'll have great fun travelling with Grandpa, whom she missed so much.'

'But I don't want Grandma to go. I want her to stay with us.'

'We can't be selfish. We have to let Grandma go. She will always be around us in spirit. Every time you do a good deed you know Grandma is there with you!' Said Mommy.

They sat down to dinner. The table was loaded with food. Oliver loved the chocolate cupcakes Aunt Sophie had baked. They tasted just like Grandma's.

And then Daddy told him all about Grandma's new adventure. How she was now racing across the heavens in her shiny new star.

Oliver listened, fascinated.

'Is Grandma already riding her star, Daddy?' Oliver asked.

'Yes, she is. Come let's go and wave at her,' Daddy said.

They walked out into the garden and looked up at the beautiful starlit sky.

Daddy pointed out to a bright big star and said, 'The one that twinkles the most is Grandma's star.'

They both waved at it. Suddenly they saw that bright star shoot across the sky.

Daddy pointed at it saying, 'Look, that's Grandma riding her star!'